This is a work of fiction. Similarities to real people, places, or events are entirely coincidental.

WHISPERS OF THE HEART EMBRACING THE FUTURE

First edition. June 4, 2024.

ISBN: 979-8224252114

Written by Candy Christie.

Whispers of the Heart

Embracing the future

Author

Candy Christie is a passionate storyteller and a fresh voice in the world of romantic fiction. With a knack for creating emotionally engaging and deeply human characters, Candy's novels explore the complexities of love, relationships, and personal growth. Drawing from her own experiences and observations of the world around her, Candy weaves intricate plots that capture the hearts of her readers.

A new author on the scene, Candy Christie has quickly gained a loyal following with her captivating Forbidden Love series. Her ability to blend romance with elements of suspense and spiritual exploration sets her work apart, creating a unique and compelling reading experience.

When she's not writing, Candy enjoys exploring nature, practicing meditation, and spending quality time with her family and friends. She believes in the transformative power of love and hopes to inspire her readers to embrace their own journeys with an open heart.

"Whispers of the Heart: Embracing the Future" is the third and final installment of the Forbidden Love series, and Candy is excited to share this concluding chapter with her readers.

Disclaimer

This book is a work of fiction. Names, characters, businesses, places, events, and incidents are either the products of the author's imagination or used in a fictitious manner. Any resemblance to actual persons, living or dead, or actual events is purely coincidental.

The author does not endorse or encourage any of the behaviors or actions depicted in this book. The story is meant for entertainment purposes only and should not be taken as advice or guidance for personal relationships. The depictions of meditation, Tantra practices, and counseling are fictional and should not replace professional guidance or treatment.

Readers are advised that this book contains mature themes and is intended for an adult audience. The author and publisher are not responsible for any actions taken by readers because of reading this book.

Thank you for respecting the author's work.

Preface

Love is a journey filled with twists and turns, joys and sorrows, and moments of profound connection. In the final installment of the Forbidden Love series, "Whispers of the Heart: Embracing the Future," we explore the deepening bond between Emily and James as they navigate the complexities of their relationship and embrace a future filled with hope and possibilities.

This series began with "Eclipsed by Desire," where Emily and James's lives were upended by unexpected passions and revelations. It continued in "Beyond the Eclipse: Exploring New Horizons," where they confronted their pasts and discovered new depths in their relationship. Now, in this concluding chapter, they face their greatest challenges yet, striving to build a life together that is both spiritually fulfilling and passionately alive.

Through trials and tribulations, Emily and James have learned that love requires honesty, vulnerability, and an unwavering commitment to each other. They have faced temptations and betrayals, yet their love has emerged stronger, forged in the fires of adversity.

In "Whispers of the Heart: Embracing the Future," we delve into their journey of healing and renewal. We witness their struggles and triumphs as they work through their issues, seek counseling, and practice Tantra meditation, finding a new spiritual connection that brings them closer than ever before. Their story is a testament to the power of love and the resilience of the human spirit.

As you turn the pages of this book, may you be inspired by Emily and James's unwavering devotion to each other. May their story remind you that true love is not without its challenges, but it is through facing these challenges together that we discover the profound depths of our hearts.

Thank you for joining Emily and James on their journey. May their whispers of the heart resonate with you and inspire you to embrace your own future with love, hope, and endless possibilities.

Warmest regards,

Candy Christie

Chapter 1: Homecoming Reality

As the first light of dawn broke over Seattle, James sat at the small desk in his hotel room, gazing out the window at the city skyline. It was his last day in Seattle, and he was wrapping up some final work tasks before heading home. His phone buzzed, and he saw Lisa's name flash on the screen.

"Hey, Lisa," James greeted, trying to keep his tone casual. "What's up?"

"Hey, James. I was wondering if we could meet up today? I have something important to discuss," Lisa's voice sounded hesitant yet urgent.

"I'm working from my hotel today, so you can drop by anytime," James replied. "I'm at the Westin, room 1208."

"Thanks, James. I'll be there soon," Lisa said before hanging up.

James felt a pang of anxiety as he ended the call. He couldn't help but worry about what Lisa needed to discuss, especially given the recent tension back home.

Back at the house, Emily and Sarah were busy settling back into their routines. The cozy home was filled with the aroma of freshly brewed coffee and the sound of light chatter. The sun streamed through the kitchen windows, casting a warm glow on the wooden floors.

"Emily, do you think we should rearrange the living room?" Sarah asked, a hint of excitement in her voice as she sipped her coffee. "I feel like a fresh start deserves a fresh look."

Emily smiled, appreciating Sarah's enthusiasm. "I think that's a great idea. Let's make this place truly ours."

They spent the morning rearranging furniture, hanging new artwork, and adding personal touches to the space. The atmosphere was filled with a sense of renewal and hope. By noon, the living room looked transformed, a perfect blend of their personalities and tastes.

Meanwhile, at the hotel, Lisa knocked on James's door. He opened it, greeting her with a warm smile. "Hey, Lisa. Come on in."

Lisa stepped inside, glancing around nervously. She wore a stylish yet casual outfit, her usual confidence slightly dimmed. "Thanks for seeing me, James."

"Of course. What's going on?" James asked, gesturing for her to sit on the couch.

Lisa took a deep breath before speaking. "James, I'm in a bit of a financial bind. My sugar daddy stopped supporting me, and I'm struggling to make ends meet. I was hoping you could help me out, but please, don't tell Sarah. She wouldn't understand."

James frowned, concern etched on his face. "Lisa, why didn't you tell me sooner? Of course, I'll help you. But you know keeping secrets can complicate things."

"I know," Lisa admitted, her eyes welling up with tears. "I just didn't know who else to turn to."

James nodded, his heart heavy. "I'll transfer some money to your account today. But you have to promise me you'll find a more stable solution soon."

"I will. Thank you, James," Lisa said, relief washing over her features. "You're a lifesaver."

James had always had a thing for Lisa, Sarah's younger sister. She was petite and curvy, with long brown hair and big brown eyes that seemed to sparkle with mischief. James had known her for years, but it wasn't until recently that he had started to see her in a different light.

When she arrived, she was looking sexy as hell in a short skirt and a tight top. They made small talk for a few minutes, but James could tell she was feeling a little uncomfortable. James decided to take a chance and put my arm around her. She tensed up at first, but then she relaxed and leaned into him.

Without thinking, James leaned in and kissed Lisa deeply, his tongue exploring her mouth. Lisa responded eagerly, moaning softly as she wrapped her arms around his neck.

"I've wanted to do that for so long," James whispered, his breath hot against Lisa's ear.

"Me too," Lisa replied, her voice husky with desire.

James's hands began to wander, caressing Lisa's body as they continued to kiss. He slipped his hand under her shirt, his fingers tracing circles around her nipples. Lisa arched her back, her breath hitching as she felt James's touch.

"You like that?" James asked, his voice low and seductive.

"Yes," Lisa moaned, her hips grinding against his.

James's hand continued to explore Lisa's body, sliding down her pants and into her panties. He slipped a finger inside her, feeling her wetness.

"You're so wet for me," James said, his voice filled with desire.

"Yes, I am," Lisa replied, her eyes shining with lust.

James continued to finger Lisa, his fingers moving in and out of her as she moaned with pleasure. He could feel her getting closer and closer to orgasm, her muscles tightening around his fingers.

"Come for me, Lisa," James whispered, his lips pressed against her ear.

Lisa did, her body shaking with pleasure as she came hard around James's fingers.

"That was amazing," Lisa said, her voice filled with satisfaction.

James smiled, his fingers still inside her.

"There's more where that came from," he said, his voice filled with promise.

Lisa looked at him, her eyes shining with desire.

"Show me," she said, her voice low and seductive.

James didn't need to be asked twice. He stood up, pulling Lisa with him. He led her to the bed, his hands exploring her body as they walked.

James pushed Lisa onto the bed. He climbed on top of her, his lips finding hers once again. They kissed deeply, their tongues exploring each other's mouths.

James's hands continued to wander, caressing Lisa's body as they kissed. He slipped his hand under her shirt, his fingers tracing circles around her nipples. Lisa arched her back, her breath hitching as she felt James's touch.

James's mouth followed his hands, his lips closing around Lisa's nipples. He sucked and bit gently, causing Lisa to moan with pleasure.

"Yes, James, just like that," Lisa said, her voice filled with desire. James continued to suck and bite Lisa's nipples, his fingers moving down to her panties. He slipped a finger inside her, feeling her wetness.

"You're so wet for me," James said, his voice low and seductive.

"Yes, I am," Lisa replied, her hips grinding against his fingers.

James's fingers moved in and out of Lisa, his thumb rubbing her clit. Lisa moaned with pleasure, her body writhing underneath him.

"I want to taste you," James said, his voice filled with desire.

Lisa nodded, her eyes shining with lust. James moved down her body, his lips leaving a trail of kisses as he went. He reached her panties, his fingers hooking around the waistband. He pulled them down, revealing Lisa's wet pussy.

James's tongue darted out, licking Lisa's pussy from bottom to top. Lisa moaned with pleasure, her hips grinding against his face. James licked and sucked, his tongue exploring every inch of Lisa's pussy.

"Yes, James, just like that," Lisa said, her voice filled with desire.

James continued to eat Lisa, his tongue moving in and out of her. He could feel her getting closer and closer to orgasm, her muscles tightening around his fingers.

"Come for me, Lisa," James whispered, his lips pressed against her clit.

Lisa did, her body shaking with pleasure as she came hard against James's face.

"That was amazing," Lisa said, her voice filled with satisfaction.

James smiled, his lips still wet with her juices.

"I'm not done with you yet," he said, his voice filled with desire.

Lisa looked at him, her eyes shining with lust.

"Show me," she said, her voice low and seductive.

James stood up, pulling Lisa with him. He led her to the edge of the bed, bending her over. He pulled her pants and panties down, revealing her ass.

James's fingers traced circles around Lisa's ass, causing her to moan with pleasure. He leaned down, his lips pressing against her ass. He kissed and licked, his tongue exploring every inch of her ass.

"Yes, James, just like that," Lisa moaned, her hips grinding against his face.

James's fingers moved down to Lisa's pussy, finding her wet again. He slipped a finger inside her, feeling her wetness.

"You're so wet for me," James said, his voice low and seductive.

"Yes, I am," Lisa replied, her hips grinding against his fingers.

James's fingers moved in and out of Lisa, his thumb rubbing her clit. Lisa moaned with pleasure, her body writhing underneath him.

"I want to fuck you," James said, his voice filled with desire.

Lisa nodded, her eyes shining with lust. James positioned himself behind her, his cock pressing against her pussy. He pushed inside her, feeling her tightness.

"Yes, James, just like that," Lisa moaned, her hips grinding against his.

James started to fuck Lisa, his hips moving back and forth. He grabbed her hips, pulling her back against him. Lisa moaned with pleasure, her body writhing underneath him.

"Fuck me harder, James," Lisa said, her voice filled with desire.

James increased his pace, fucking Lisa harder and faster. Lisa moaned with pleasure, her body shaking with every thrust.

"Yes, James, just like that," Lisa moaned, her hips grinding against his.

James could feel himself getting closer and closer to orgasm, his balls tightening.

"I'm going to come," James said, his voice filled with desire.

"Come inside me," Lisa said, her voice low and seductive.

James did, his body shaking with pleasure as he came inside Lisa.

"That was amazing," Lisa said, her voice filled with satisfaction.

James pulled out of her, his cock still hard.

"I'm not done with you yet," he said, his voice filled with desire.

Lisa looked at him, her eyes shining with lust.

"Show me," she said, her voice low and seductive.

They kissed deeply, their tongues exploring each other's mouths. James's cock pressed against Lisa's pussy, sliding inside her. He started to fuck her, his hips moving back and forth. Lisa moaned with pleasure, her hips grinding against his.

"Yes, James, just like that," Lisa moaned, her hands running through his hair.

James continued to fuck Lisa, his hips moving back and forth. He could feel himself getting closer and closer to orgasm, his balls tightening.

"I'm going to come," James said, his voice filled with desire.

"Come inside me," Lisa said, her voice low and seductive.

James did, his body shaking with pleasure as he came inside Lisa.

"That was amazing," Lisa said, her voice filled with satisfaction.

James collapsed on top of her, his body spent.

"I told you I wasn't done with you yet," he said, his voice filled with satisfaction.

Lisa laughed, her hands running through his hair.

"I'm glad you weren't, can we do it again" she said, her voice filled with desire.

James smiled and kissed her. "Anytime, Lisa. Anytime."

"You're so beautiful," he murmured, looking into her eyes.

"And you're not so bad yourself," Lisa replied, running her hand through James's hair.

They lay there for a while, enjoying each other's company and the feeling of skin on skin. But after a while, the tension began to build again. Lisa reached down and started stroking James's cock, which was already starting to harden.

"Mmm, I think someone's ready for round two," she said with a grin.

James rolled on top of Lisa and they started kissing again, their tongues exploring each other's mouths. Lisa wrapped her legs around James's waist, pulling him closer.

"Fuck me, James," she whispered in his ear. "I want to feel you inside me again."

James didn't need any further encouragement. He positioned himself at Lisa's entrance and slowly pushed inside her. They both moaned as he filled her up, his cock hitting all the right spots.

"Yes, just like that," Lisa said, digging her nails into James's back.

James started thrusting in and out of Lisa, building up a steady rhythm. Lisa matched his movements, grinding her hips against his. They were both lost in the pleasure of the moment, their moans and gasps filling the room.

"Oh, fuck, Lisa," James said, his breath coming in short bursts. "You feel so good."

"Don't stop, James," Lisa begged. "I'm so close."

James picked up the pace, his thrusts becoming more urgent. Lisa could feel herself on the brink of orgasm, her muscles tensing up.

"Yes, yes, yes!" she cried out as she came, her pussy clenching around James's cock.

James wasn't far behind. With a few more thrusts, he came too, filling Lisa with his hot cum.

They lay there for a few moments, catching their breath. James rolled off Lisa and they cuddled up together.

"That was amazing," Lisa said, snuggling closer to James.

"Yeah, it was," James agreed, kissing the top of Lisa's head.

They lay there in silence for a while, their bodies entwined. But after a while, Lisa's hand started wandering again, tracing circles on James's chest.

"You know, I'm not done with you yet," she said with a sly smile.

James grinned. "Oh, really? And what do you have in mind?"

Lisa leaned in and whispered her idea in James's ear. He groaned with pleasure at the thought.

"I think I like where this is going," he said, pulling Lisa closer.

And with that, they began round three, their bodies moving together in a dance as old as time.

Back at home, Emily and Sarah took a break from their work, settling on the newly arranged couch. They were both dressed in comfortable jeans and sweaters, their faces glowing with satisfaction from their hard work.

"Do you think James will like it?" Sarah asked, a hint of uncertainty in her voice.

Emily took Sarah's hand, giving it a reassuring squeeze. "He'll love it. It's a reflection of us and the life we're building together."

They sat in comfortable silence for a moment, enjoying the peace and the warmth of the afternoon sun streaming through the windows.

"What do you think the future holds for us?" Sarah asked softly, her eyes fixed on the horizon.

Emily pondered for a moment before responding. "I think it will be challenging at times, but as long as we communicate and support each other, we'll be okay. We need to be honest about our feelings and work together."

Sarah nodded, feeling a sense of reassurance. "You're right. We've come this far, and I believe we can handle whatever comes our way."

As the afternoon turned to evening, they prepared a simple yet delicious dinner, setting the table with care. The kitchen was filled with the comforting smells of home-cooked food and the sound of laughter and conversation.

When James finally returned, he was greeted by the sight of his transformed home and the loving faces of Emily and Sarah. His heart swelled with gratitude and love.

"Wow, you two have been busy," James said, taking in the changes. "It looks amazing."

"Do you like it?" Emily asked, her eyes sparkling with anticipation.

"I love it," James replied, pulling both women into a warm embrace. "It's perfect, just like us."

As they sat down to dinner, they talked about their plans and dreams, sharing their hopes for the future. The atmosphere was filled with love and a sense of unity, as they faced the reality of their situation together, stronger than ever.

After a delicious dinner, the three of them settled on the couch to watch their favorite TV show. Max, soon joined them, snuggling up between James and Emily. Sarah, sitting on the other side of James, couldn't help but notice how handsome he looked after his time away.

As the night went on, Max's eyelids grew heavier and heavier until he finally fell asleep. Emily, sensing that it was time, gave Sarah a knowing look and the two of them led James to their bedroom.

As they entered the room, She had always had a crush on James, and now that she was with James, she couldn't believe what was happening. Emily, noticing Sarah, took her hand and gave it a squeeze.

James, still thinking of Sarah as Lisa, sat down on the bed and pulled her close. He could feel her heart racing as he leaned in for a kiss. Sarah, unable to resist, melted into his arms, her body responding to his touch.

As they explored each other's bodies, their moans filled the room. James' hands roamed over Sarah's curves, cupping her breasts and teasing her nipples. Sarah, unable to contain herself, let out a soft moan as James' fingers found their way to her wet and ready pussy.

"Oh, James," Sarah whispered, her breath hot against his ear. "I've wanted this for so long."

James, lost in the moment, didn't even realize that he had been calling Sarah by the wrong name. He was too caught up in the heat of the moment to care. He leaned in for another kiss, his tongue exploring Sarah's mouth as his fingers continued to work their magic. Emily was confused with another name James mentioned and did not actively engage in the act today.

Sarah, unable to hold back any longer, climbed on top of James, straddling him. She could feel his hard cock pressing against her wet pussy, begging to be let in. She slowly lowered herself onto him, letting out a soft moan as he filled her up.

As they moved together, Sarah's moans grew louder and louder. James, lost in the moment, couldn't help but let out a few moans of his own. The bed creaked beneath them as they moved faster and faster, their bodies slick with sweat.

"Oh, James, yes," Sarah moaned, her nails digging into his shoulders. "Harder, harder."

James, happy to oblige, thrust into her harder and harder, their bodies slapping together. Sarah's moans grew louder and louder until she finally let out a loud scream as she reached her peak. James, unable to hold back any longer, followed her over the edge, his cock pulsing inside of her as he filled her up with his cum.

As they lay there, panting and spent, Sarah couldn't help but feel a little disappointed. She had always dreamed of this moment, but she never thought it would be with James calling her by someone else's name. But as she looked into his eyes, she knew that it didn't matter. She was with the love of her life that she had always longed for, and that was all that mattered.

Despite the secrets and challenges that lay ahead, in that moment, they felt truly happy and content, ready to embrace whatever the future held for them.

Chapter 2: Balancing Acts

As the sun rose over their suburban home, Emily stood in the kitchen, preparing breakfast. The aroma of freshly brewed coffee and sizzling bacon filled the air. She wore a simple dress, her hair pulled back into a loose ponytail, a look of determination on her face as she set the table. Sarah breezed into the kitchen, dressed in a fashionable outfit, ready for another day of pampering and leisure activities.

"Morning, Em," Sarah greeted, grabbing a cup of coffee. "Thanks for making breakfast."

"Morning," Emily replied, forcing a smile. "Just trying to keep everything in order."

James entered the kitchen, his presence filling the room with a warm, comforting energy. He kissed Emily on the cheek and then Sarah, their morning routine now a familiar dance.

"Smells great in here," James said, taking his seat at the table. "What's the plan for today?"

"I'm heading to the spa and then meeting a friend for lunch," Sarah said, her eyes sparkling with excitement.

"I'll be taking Max to his soccer practice and then running some errands," Emily replied, trying to keep her voice steady. She couldn't shake the feeling of unease that had settled in since the previous day's conversation about Lisa.

"Sounds like a full day," James said, looking between the two women. "I'll be home late, so don't wait up for me."

After breakfast, Emily took Max to his soccer practice. She watched him run across the field, his laughter echoing in the air. Despite the joy of seeing her son happy, her mind kept drifting back to the name James had mentioned. She was certain he was meeting someone else and couldn't let it go.

When they returned home, Emily found herself doing most of the household chores. She cleaned, cooked, and took care of Max, all while Sarah was out enjoying herself. The imbalance in their responsibilities weighed heavily on her, adding to her growing frustration.

Later that evening, as Sarah was getting ready to go out again, Emily couldn't hold back her thoughts any longer.

"Sarah, I need to talk to you," Emily said, her voice tense. "I feel like I'm doing everything around here while you're out having fun."

Sarah paused, her expression softening. "I'm sorry, Emily. I didn't realize you felt that way. I'll try to help more."

"It's not just that," Emily continued, her voice trembling. "I can't stop thinking about the name James mentioned yesterday. I'm sure he's meeting someone else."

Sarah looked at her with concern. "What do you mean?"

"I think he's seeing someone behind our backs," Emily said, her eyes filling with tears. "I can't shake the feeling."

Sarah hugged her tightly. "We'll figure it out, Em. But please, don't do anything rash."

But Emily had already made up her mind. That evening, after Max was in bed and Sarah was out, Emily called Mark. She needed to feel something other than the pain and uncertainty that had taken over her heart.

"Mark, can we meet?" Emily asked, her voice barely above a whisper.

"Of course," Mark replied, sensing the urgency in her voice. "Come over to my place."

Emily drove to Mark's apartment, her mind racing with emotions. When she arrived, Mark greeted her with a concerned look.

"Emily, what's going on?" he asked, leading her inside.

"I just... I needed to see you," Emily said, tears streaming down her face. "James is meeting someone else, and I can't stand it."

Mark pulled her into a comforting embrace. "I'm here for you, Emily. Always."

They sat on the couch, talking about everything that had been happening. Mark listened patiently, offering support and understanding. As the night went on, their conversation turned into something more, a desperate need for connection and comfort.

Emily pulled off her dress, revealing her perfect curves. Mark couldn't help but stare, his cock already rock hard. Emily noticed and dropped to her knees, taking Mark's cock into her mouth.

Mark groaned as Emily deep-throated him, her lips and tongue working in perfect harmony. He tangled his fingers in her hair, pulling her closer. Emily looked up at him, her eyes full of mischief. "You like that?" she asked, before taking him even deeper.

Mark couldn't take it any longer. He pulled Emily to her feet and pushed her against the wall, his hands roaming her body. Emily moaned as he cupped her breasts, his thumbs flicking her nipples. Mark leaned in, whispering dirty thoughts in Emily's ear. "I want to eat your ass," he growled.

Emily's eyes widened, but she nodded, leading Mark to the bedroom. Mark wasted no time, burying his face between Emily's cheeks. He licked and sucked, reveling in the taste of her. Emily moaned, her hips grinding against Mark's face.

Mark couldn't resist any longer. He slipped a finger into Emily's pussy, feeling her wetness coat his hand. He added a second finger, fucking her with his hand as he continued to eat her ass. Emily's moans grew louder, her body trembling with pleasure.

Mark knew Emily was ready. He positioned himself between her legs, his cock poised at her entrance. Emily looked up at him, her eyes filled with desire. "Fuck me," she whispered. Mark didn't need to be asked twice. He thrust into her, filling her completely.

They moved together in missionary position, their bodies slick with sweat. Mark whispered dirty talk in Emily's ear, telling her how good she felt and how much he wanted her. Emily responded in kind, her nails digging into Mark's back.

As they reached their peak, Mark pulled out, his cum splattering Emily's stomach. Emily moaned, her body trembling with pleasure. Mark collapsed beside her, his heart racing. "That was amazing," he whispered. Emily smiled, her eyes filled with satisfaction. "Yes, it was."

They lay on Mark's bed, both completely naked, exploring each other's bodies with their hands.

"You're so beautiful," Mark whispered, leaning in to kiss Emily's neck. She moaned softly, running her fingers through his hair.

"Thank you Mark" she replied, pulling him closer.

Mark couldn't resist any longer. He climbed on top of Emily, positioning himself between her legs again. She wrapped her legs around his waist, pulling him closer still.

"Fuck me, Mark," she begged. "I need you inside me."

Mark didn't need any more encouragement. He entered her slowly, savoring the feeling of her warmth surrounding him. She moaned as he filled her up, digging her nails into his back.

"Harder," she gasped, urging him on.

Mark was happy to oblige. He began to thrust harder and faster, losing himself in the moment. Emily matched his rhythm, meeting him thrust for thrust.

"Yes, yes, yes!" she cried out, reaching her climax.

Mark wasn't far behind. He groaned as he came, collapsing on top of Emily.

They lay there for a few moments, catching their breath. But Mark wasn't done yet. He wanted more.

"Let's go again?" he asked, looking down at Emily.

She smiled up at him. "You bet."

This time, things were more intense. Mark was rougher, more aggressive. Emily loved it. She begged for more, urging him on.

"Yes, yes, just like that!" she cried out, as Mark pounded into her.

They switched positions, with Emily on top. She rode him hard, grinding her hips against his. Mark reached up to pinch her nipples, eliciting a moan from Emily.

"Oh, fuck, yes!" she cried out, as she came again.

Mark wasn't far behind. He grabbed Emily's hips, thrusting up into her as he came.

They collapsed onto the bed, both panting and sweaty. But Mark wasn't done yet.

"Round three?" he asked, looking over at Emily.

She smiled at him. "I thought you'd never ask."

This time, things were more adventurous. Mark suggested they try something new. Emily was hesitant at first, but she quickly warmed up to the idea.

Mark lubed up his fingers, teasing Emily's ass. She gasped as he entered her, but she quickly relaxed and began to enjoy the sensation.

Mark positioned himself behind Emily, entering her slowly. She moaned as he filled her up, reaching back to grab his hips.

"Yes, just like that," she whispered, as Mark began to thrust.

They moved together, lost in their own little world. Emily came hard, her moans filling the room. Mark followed soon after, collapsing on top of her.

They lay there, tangled up in each other's arms, completely satisfied. Emily stayed the night at Mark's place, both of them knowing that this was the start of something special.

Meanwhile, at home, James returned late, finding the house quiet and empty. He noticed Emily wasn't there but didn't think much of it, assuming she was with a friend.

The next morning, Emily returned home, feeling a mix of guilt and relief. She knew she had crossed a line, but she also felt a sense of empowerment. She couldn't let herself be consumed by doubt and fear.

"Morning," Sarah greeted her, sensing something was off. "You okay?"

"Yeah," Emily replied, forcing a smile. "Just needed some time to clear my head. I stayed with mom"

As they sat down for breakfast, Emily couldn't help but feel a renewed determination. She would confront James about her suspicions, but she wouldn't let it consume her. She had to find a balance between her responsibilities and her own needs.

Throughout the day, Emily and Sarah worked together to maintain their household, their bond growing stronger despite the underlying tensions. They knew they had to support each other if they were going to navigate the complexities of their relationship and family life.

That evening, as they sat down for dinner, James sensed the shift in the atmosphere. He looked at Emily, who met his gaze with a steely resolve.

"James, we need to talk," Emily said, her voice calm but firm.

James nodded, setting down his fork. "I know. Let's talk after dinner."

As they ate, the weight of the conversation hung over them, but they all knew it was necessary. They had to address the issues that had been simmering beneath the surface if they were going to move forward together.

After dinner, they sat in the living room, the air thick with tension. Emily took a deep breath, ready to confront the man she loved.

"James, I need to know the truth," she began. "Who are you meeting in Seattle?"

James looked at her, his expression a mix of guilt and concern. "It's not what you think, Emily. Lisa needed help, and I couldn't turn her away."

Emily's eyes widened in shock. "Lisa? Why didn't you tell us?"

"I didn't want to worry you," James explained. "She's in a tough spot, and I felt like I had to help."

Emily's anger flared, but she forced herself to stay calm. "We need to be honest with each other, James. No more secrets."

James nodded, his expression remorseful. "I promise. No more secrets."

As they sat together, Emily felt a glimmer of hope. They had a long way to go, but they were finally starting to address the issues that had been tearing them apart. With open hearts and clear communication, they could begin to heal and rebuild their lives together.

Chapter 3: Unexpected Visit

James's plane touched down in Seattle on a rainy afternoon. He felt a mix of anticipation and dread as he made his way to the hotel. The cityscape blurred by the drizzle reflected his turbulent thoughts. After checking into his room, he texted Lisa to let her know he is in Seattle for few days.

In less than an hour, there was a knock on his door. James opened it to find Lisa standing there, her expression a mix of relief and anxiety. She was dressed in a casual yet stylish outfit, but the worry lines on her face were evident.

"Hey, Lisa," James greeted, stepping aside to let her in. "Come on in."

"Thanks for seeing me, James," Lisa said, her voice soft but strained.

They sat down on the small couch in his hotel room, the muted sounds of the city outside providing a background hum. James studied her face, noticing the shadows under her eyes and the tension in her posture.

"Lisa, you said you needed to talk. What's going on?" James asked gently.

Lisa took a deep breath, her eyes welling up with tears. "I'm in trouble, James. My sugar daddy cut me off. I don't have enough to cover my bills, and I'm scared."

James's heart ached at her vulnerability. "Why didn't you tell me sooner?"

"I didn't want to be a burden," Lisa admitted, wiping away a tear. "But I don't have anyone else to turn to."

James reached out, taking her hand in his. "You're not a burden, Lisa. I told you I'd help. How much do you need?"

Lisa looked down, her voice barely above a whisper. "Two thousand dollars would help me get through the next few months."

James nodded, already calculating how he could shift some funds to help her. "I'll transfer it to you thousand tonight for now. But Lisa, you need to find a more stable solution. This isn't sustainable."

"I know," Lisa said, her voice breaking. "But it's so hard, James. I don't know what to do but this will help."

James squeezed her hand, his voice filled with compassion. "We'll figure it out together. You're not alone in this."

Lisa leaned against him, her body shaking with silent sobs. James wrapped his arms around her, offering what comfort he could. The room was filled with a heavy silence, the weight of their conversation pressing down on both of them.

"Thank you, James," Lisa said after a while, her voice hoarse. "I don't know what I'd do without you."

"You'll get through this, Lisa," James replied, his voice firm. "And I'll be here to help you every step of the way."

They sat in silence for a while, each lost in their own thoughts. James couldn't shake the guilt he felt for keeping this from Emily and Sarah, but he also knew he couldn't abandon Lisa in her time of need.

"James, can I ask you something?" Lisa said, breaking the silence.

"Of course," James replied, looking at her intently.

"Why are you helping me?" Lisa asked, her eyes searching his.

James sighed, running a hand through his hair. "Because I care about you, Lisa. You're Sarah's sister, and you're important to me too. I don't want to see you suffer."

Lisa nodded, tears welling up again. "Thank you. That means a lot to me."

"Lisa, I have to go for shower since I did not take it in the morning" he whispered, his voice low and full of longing.

"I also did not since I was in a rush to come here, can I join you? I give a good back rub." she replied, her voice barely above a whisper.

James was ecstatic took a step closer to her, their bodies almost touching. She looked up at him, her eyes filled with desire. He leaned in, capturing her lips with his in a passionate kiss.

Their tongues danced together as they explored each other's mouths. James's hands wandered down Lisa's body, cupping her ass and pulling her closer to him.

"I want you, Lisa," he murmured against her lips.

"I want you too, James," she replied, her voice husky with desire.

Without breaking their kiss, James picked Lisa up and carried her to the shower. He turned on the water, adjusting the temperature to a comfortable warmth.

They stepped under the spray, their bodies slick with water and desire. James's hands roamed over Lisa's wet skin, his fingers tracing the curve of her breasts and the length of her legs.

Lisa moaned as James's fingers found her clit, rubbing slow circles over the sensitive bundle of nerves. She arched her back, pressing her breasts against his chest.

James's mouth found Lisa's earlobe, his teeth nipping at the delicate skin. She gasped, her breath hitching in her throat as pleasure coursed through her body.

"James," she murmured, her voice full of longing.

He lifted her up, pinning her against the shower wall. She wrapped her legs around his waist, her pussy wet and ready for him.

James thrust into her, filling her completely. She moaned, her head falling back against the wall as he started to move inside her.

Their bodies moved together in a rhythm as old as time itself. James's fingers found Lisa's clit again, rubbing slow circles as he fucked her harder and harder.

Lisa moaned, her breath coming in short gasps as she felt herself getting close to the edge.

"James, I'm going to cum," she cried out, her voice full of need.

James thrust into her harder, his fingers moving faster over her clit. Lisa's orgasm crashed over her, her pussy clenching around his cock as she came hard.

James groaned, his cock twitching inside her as he felt his own orgasm building. He pulled out, his cum spilling out of Lisa's pussy and down her thighs.

Without hesitation, James knelt down and licked Lisa's pussy, tasting her cum and his own. Lisa moaned, her hands buried in his hair as he licked and sucked her clit.

"James, what are you doing?" she asked, her voice full of surprise.

"Ass to mouth, Lisa," he replied, his voice muffled by her pussy.

Lisa gasped as James's tongue delved into her ass, licking and probing the tight hole. She moaned, her body trembling with pleasure as he tongued her ass.

James stood up, his cock hard and ready again. He turned Lisa around, bending her over and entering her from behind.

Lisa moaned, her body moving back to meet his thrusts. James's fingers found her clit again, rubbing slow circles as he fucked her hard and deep.

They moved together, their bodies slick with water and sweat. Lisa moaned, her orgasm building again as James's fingers worked their magic.

"James, I'm going to cum again," she cried out, her voice full of need.

James thrust into her harder, his fingers moving faster over her clit. Lisa's orgasm crashed over her, her pussy clenching around his cock as she came hard.

James groaned, his cock twitching inside her as he felt his own orgasm building. He pulled out, his cum spilling out of Lisa's pussy and down her thighs.

Without hesitation, Lisa knelt down and took James's cock in her mouth, swallowing his cum as he groaned with pleasure.

They stood there, their bodies slick with water and sweat, their breaths coming in short gasps.

"I love you, Lisa," James whispered, his voice full of emotion.

"I love you too, James," Lisa replied, her voice full of longing.

They stood there, their bodies entwined, their hearts beating as one. The forbidden love that had brought them together was still burning bright, fueled by their passion and desire.

They spent the rest of the afternoon talking, James offering advice and support while Lisa opened up about her fears and struggles. As the rain continued to fall outside, they found solace in each other's company, both feeling a little less alone in the world.

By the time Lisa left, the tension in the room had eased somewhat. James watched her go, his heart heavy with the knowledge of the secret he was keeping. He knew he needed to tell Emily and Sarah eventually, but for now, he focused on helping Lisa find her footing.

As he closed the door behind her, James couldn't shake the feeling that their lives were becoming increasingly complicated. But he also knew that as long as they faced these challenges together, they could find a way through the storm.

Chapter 4: Secrets Unveiled

The sun was setting, casting a warm golden hue over the house as Emily sat at the kitchen table, her mind racing. She had noticed subtle changes in James's behavior over the past few weeks. He seemed distant, preoccupied, and his frequent trips to Seattle were becoming a point of concern. She knew she couldn't ignore it any longer.

James walked into the kitchen, loosening his tie, his face weary from the day. "Hey, Em," he greeted, leaning down to kiss her cheek. "What's for dinner?"

"James, we need to talk," Emily said, her voice steady but serious. She looked up at him, her eyes filled with concern.

James froze, sensing the gravity of her words. He pulled out a chair and sat down across from her. "What's going on?"

Emily took a deep breath, gathering her thoughts. "I've noticed you've been different lately. You're distant, and you've been making a lot of trips to Seattle. What's really going on, James?"

James sighed, running a hand through his hair. "Emily, it's not what you think. Its office work and also, I've been helping Lisa."

Emily's eyes widened in surprise. "Lisa? Why didn't you tell me?"

James looked down; guilt etched on his face. "She asked me not to. She's in a tough spot, Em. Her employer cut her off, and she doesn't have anyone else to turn to."

Emily's mind raced, processing the information. "So, you've been giving her money? That's why you've been going to Seattle?"

James nodded, his voice filled with regret. "I should have told you. I'm sorry. I didn't want to worry you."

Emily felt a mix of emotions – relief that he wasn't having an affair, but also frustration and hurt that he had kept this from her. "James, I understand wanting to help Lisa, but keeping this from me... it's not okay. We need to be honest with each other."

James reached out, taking her hand in his. "You're right, Emily. I'm sorry. I should have told you from the beginning. I just didn't want to add more stress to your plate."

Emily squeezed his hand, her eyes softening. "We're in this together, James. We need to face these things as a team. No more secrets."

James nodded, his eyes filled with sincerity. "No more secrets. I promise."

The atmosphere in the kitchen was tense but filled with a sense of resolution. Emily felt a weight lift off her shoulders, knowing the truth. But she also knew there was still a lot to work through.

That night, as they lay in bed, Emily couldn't shake the feeling of unease. She trusted James, but the fact that he had kept this from her gnawed at her. She turned to him, her voice a whisper in the darkness. "James, promise me we'll always be honest with each other from now on."

James pulled her close, his voice filled with emotion. "I promise, Emily. No more secrets."

Meanwhile, in Seattle, Lisa sat alone in her apartment, staring at her phone. She felt a pang of guilt for dragging James into her problems, but she also felt a glimmer of hope knowing she had someone to rely on. She knew she needed to find a way to stand on her own feet, but for now, she was grateful for James's support.

The next morning, Emily woke up early, her mind still restless. She decided to call Sarah and share what had happened. She needed to talk to someone, to process everything.

"Hey, Sarah," Emily said when her Sarah answered. "Do you have a minute? I need to talk."

"Of course, Em. What's going on?" Sarah replied, her voice filled with concern.

Emily took a deep breath and recounted the events of the previous night. Sarah listened patiently, offering words of comfort and advice.

"You did the right thing, Emily. Communication is key. And it sounds like James really wants to make things right," Sarah said.

"I know," Emily sighed. "It's just hard to wrap my head around everything."

Sarah's voice was gentle. "Take it one step at a time. You're strong, Emily. You'll get through this."

Emily felt a sense of relief talking to Sarah. She knew she wasn't alone in this, and that gave her the strength to move forward.

As the days passed, Emily and James worked on rebuilding their trust. They spent more time together, talking openly about their feelings and concerns. James made an effort to be more present, and Emily slowly started to feel more secure in their relationship.

One evening, as they sat on the porch watching the sunset, Emily turned to James. "I know things have been tough, but I believe we can get through this. We just need to keep communicating."

James nodded; his eyes filled with determination. "I agree. We've come this far, and I'm not giving up on us."

They sat in silence for a while, enjoying the peaceful evening. Emily felt a sense of hope, knowing that they were taking the right steps to heal and move forward. She leaned her head on James's shoulder, feeling a renewed sense of connection.

"Thank you for being honest with me," Emily said softly.

James kissed the top of her head. "Thank you for understanding. I love you, Emily."

"I love you too, James," she replied, her heart full of emotion.

James had always found his wife Emily to be incredibly alluring, but tonight, something was different. She was radiating an energy that he couldn't resist. As they sat on the couch, he leaned in, whispering in her ear, "Emily, you look absolutely stunning tonight."

Emily blushed, her cheeks turning a soft pink. "Why, thank you, James," she replied, her voice husky with desire.

James took a moment to trace his fingers along Emily's earlobe, feeling her shiver beneath his touch. "You know, I can't stop thinking about how good you taste," he murmured, his breath hot against her skin.

Emily's breath hitched as James's lips found hers, his tongue exploring her mouth with a passion that made her heart race. She moaned softly, her hands reaching up to tangle in his hair.

"Take me to bed, James," she whispered, her voice filled with need.

James didn't need to be told twice. He scooped Emily up in his arms, carrying her to their bedroom. Once there, he laid her down on the bed, his eyes raking over her body with a hunger that made her squirm.

"God, Emily, you're so beautiful," he said, his voice thick with desire.

Emily smiled, her hands reaching out to undo James's belt. "Then show me how much you want me," she said, her voice filled with challenge.

James didn't hesitate. He stripped off his clothes, his eyes never leaving Emily's. Once he was naked, he climbed onto the bed, his body hovering over hers.

"Like this?" he asked, his lips finding Emily's earlobe once again.

Emily moaned, her body arching towards James. "Yes, just like that," she said, her hands reaching up to tangle in his hair.

James began to kiss his way down Emily's body, his lips and tongue leaving a trail of fire in their wake. When he reached her breasts, he took one nipple into his mouth, sucking and nibbling until Emily was writhing beneath him.

"James, please," she begged, her hands reaching down to grip his hips.

James knew what Emily wanted, and he was more than happy to give it to her. He moved down her body, his tongue dipping into her navel before continuing down to her wet and waiting core.

"Oh, James," Emily moaned, her legs spreading wide to give him better access.

James took his time, licking and sucking at Emily's clit until she was on the brink of orgasm. Only then did he slide a finger inside of her, curling it up to hit her G-spot.

Emily's orgasm hit her like a wave, her body shaking and trembling as James continued to lick and suck at her clit. When she finally came down from her high, she looked up at James with a lazy smile.

"That was incredible," she said, her voice filled with satisfaction.

James grinned, crawling up her body to kiss her deeply. "I'm not done with you yet," he said, his voice filled with promise.

Emily's eyes sparkled with desire as James positioned himself at her entrance. "Then show me," she said, her hands reaching down to grip his hips.

James slid inside of Emily slowly, savoring the feeling of her tight walls surrounding him. Once he was fully seated, he began to move, his hips rocking back and forth in a steady rhythm.

"Oh, James, yes," Emily moaned, her nails digging into his hips.

James leaned down to capture Emily's lips in a deep kiss, their tongues dancing together as their bodies moved in perfect harmony.

As their pleasure built, James reached down to grip Emily's hips, changing the angle of his thrusts. Emily's moans grew louder, her body trembling with the effort of holding back her orgasm.

"Come for me, Emily," James whispered in her ear, his voice filled with desire.

Emily's orgasm hit her like a tidal wave, her body shaking and trembling as James continued to thrust into her. When she finally came down from her high, she looked up at James with a lazy smile.

"That was amazing," she said, her voice filled with satisfaction and thinking how her life has changed in last few months from almost divorce to best romantic days of her life, thus far.

James grinned, collapsing next to her on the bed. "I'm glad you enjoyed yourself," he said, his voice filled with pride.

Emily snuggled up against him, her head resting on his chest. "I always do when I'm with you," she said, her voice filled with love.

James wrapped his arms around Emily, holding her close. "I love you, Emily," he said, his voice filled with emotion.

Emily looked up at James, her eyes shining with love. "I love you too, James," she said, her voice filled with emotion.

As they lay there, wrapped up in each other's arms, the world outside faded away, leaving only the two of them and their love for each other.

Chapter 5: A New Proposal

Sarah paced around her apartment, her mind racing with anticipation and anxiety. She had reached out to an old lover, a multimillionaire named Steve, to fund her startup idea. Steve had been intrigued and agreed to meet her to discuss the project. They had met several times that week, and today was the day he would give her his final decision.

The doorbell rang, breaking her train of thought. She took a deep breath and opened the door to find Steve standing there, looking as composed as ever. He wore a tailored suit that highlighted his status and confidence.

"Sarah," Steve greeted, his voice smooth and warm. "It's good to see you."

"Steve," Sarah replied, trying to keep her voice steady. "Come in."

They sat on the couch, the room filled with the soft light of the late afternoon sun filtering through the curtains. Sarah wore a simple yet elegant dress, her hair cascading over her shoulders. Steve's presence filled the room with an air of sophistication and nostalgia.

"I've gone over your proposal," Steve began, his eyes locking onto hers. "And I think it's a brilliant idea. I'm willing to invest in your startup."

Sarah's heart skipped a beat, a mixture of relief and excitement washing over her. "Steve, thank you so much. This means the world to me."

Steve reached out, taking her hand in his. "I've always believed in you, Sarah. You have a knack for seeing opportunities where others don't."

Their eyes met, and for a moment, the past and present intertwined. The memories of their time together came rushing back, filling the room with a sense of shared history and unspoken emotions.

As the week went on, Sarah found herself spending more and more time at her apartment, making excuses to Emily. She needed to finalize the details of the investment and prepare for the next steps of her startup. The excitement of her new venture was exhilarating, but it also created a distance between her and Emily.

Evening, as Sarah and Steve were wrapping up their meeting, Steve looked at her with a serious expression. "Sarah, I know we agreed to keep this professional, but I can't help but feel a connection between us. There's something still there, isn't it?"

Sarah felt a flutter in her chest, memories of their passionate past flashing before her eyes. "Steve, I... I can't deny that there's still something between us. But my life is complicated now." Sarah got up from the dining table and started going towards the living room.

Steve followed her into the living room, and they sat down on the couch. They made small talk, catching up on old times, but Steve could feel the tension building between them. He knew they both wanted the same thing.

Finally, he couldn't take it anymore. He leaned in and kissed her, and Sarah responded eagerly. They moved to the bedroom, their clothes coming off as they kissed and touched each other.

"I've missed you so much," Steve murmured, as he kissed her neck.

"I've missed you too, but my life is complicated right now." Sarah replied, as she ran her hands over his chest.

Steve started to kiss her breasts, taking each nipple into his mouth and teasing it with his tongue. Sarah moaned, and tried to resist and push him away, unwillingly. He moved down further, kissing her stomach and then her thighs.

He spread her legs apart and started to lick her pussy, making her moan louder. He teased her clit with his tongue, and Sarah grabbed his head, pushing him away.

"No, Steve, No," she moaned, as she came hard.

Sarahs reluctance made Steve more excited. Steve moved up and entered her, and they started to fuck, hard and fast. Sarah still saying no at every thrust wrapped her legs around him, and Steve could feel her pussy gripping his cock.

"Please don't fuck me, Steve, No, no" Sarah begged, as she came again and again.

Steve could feel himself getting close, and he pulled out, shooting his load all over Sarah's stomach. She smiled, and Steve leaned down to kiss her.

"I've missed you so much," he said again, as they cuddled together.

"I've missed you too, but this is not right. I am with someone else now" Sarah replied, as they lay naked next to each other, satisfied.

Meanwhile, back at home, Emily was feeling increasingly lonely. James had gone on a trip to Vegas with his friends, and to make matters worse, Lisa had also planned a trip to Vegas. Emily found herself alone in the house, the silence amplifying her feelings of isolation.

She tried to keep herself busy, taking care of the household chores and spending time with Max, but the emptiness gnawed at her. One evening, as she sat on the porch with a cup of tea, she called Sarah.

"Hey, Sarah," Emily said, trying to keep her voice light. "How's everything going with your project?"

"It's going well, Em," Sarah replied, her voice sounding distant as she lay naked next to Steve. "Just a lot of hard work to get through."

"I miss you," Emily admitted, her voice soft. "The house feels empty without you and James."

Sarah felt a pang of guilt. She missed Emily too, but she was so caught up with Steve in her new venture and the emotions stirred by Steve's presence. Steve, caressing her breasts. "I miss you too, Em. I'll be home soon, I promise."

After hanging up, Emily felt a sense of longing. She couldn't shake the feeling that something was changing between them. She decided to reach out to Mark, needing someone to talk to and maybe distract her from her loneliness.

"Mark, can we meet up?" Emily texted, her fingers trembling slightly.

"Of course, Emily. Anytime you need," Mark replied.

They met at a quiet café, the familiar surroundings bringing a sense of comfort. Mark listened as Emily poured out her feelings, offering support and understanding. As they talked, Emily felt a sense of connection, a reminder that she wasn't completely alone.

Back at Sarah's apartment, Steve was preparing to leave. "Sarah, if you ever need anything, you know where to find me," he said, his voice sincere.

"Thank you, Steve," Sarah replied dressing up, her heart heavy with conflicting emotions. "I appreciate everything you've done for me."

As Steve left, Sarah sat down on the couch, feeling a mix of triumph, guilt and uncertainty. She had secured the funding for her startup, but the interactions with Steve had stirred up old feelings and complicated her emotions.

Sarah couldn't believe it. After the meeting with Steve, she couldn't wait to tell Emily about the potential investment opportunity. She rushed home, her mind racing with excitement.

Emily was in the kitchen when Sarah arrived, cooking dinner for the two of them. Sarah wrapped her arms around Emily's waist and planted a kiss on her neck. "Hey, love," Emily said, turning to face Sarah.

"Hey," Sarah replied, her eyes sparkling with excitement. "I have some news."

Emily raised an eyebrow. "Oh?"

Sarah told Emily about her meeting with Steve, and the investment opportunity he had presented. Emily listened intently, her eyes lighting up with excitement as Sarah spoke.

"Wow, that's amazing," Emily said when Sarah finished. "We could do so much with that kind of money."

Sarah nodded. "I know. I think we should do it."

Emily wrapped her arms around Sarah's neck and pulled her in for a kiss. "Then let's do it," she said.

As they ate dinner, Sarah and Emily chatted excitedly about their plans. They talked about the different ways they could invest the money, and the impact it could have on their lives.

After dinner, they moved to the living room and continued their conversation. Sarah sat on the couch, her legs tucked under her, while Emily sat on the floor in front of her.

As they talked, Sarah's hand drifted to Emily's hair, absentmindedly playing with the strands. Emily leaned into Sarah's touch, her eyes never leaving Sarah's face.

Suddenly, Sarah leaned down and pressed her lips to Emily's. Emily responded eagerly, her arms snaking around Sarah's waist.

Their kiss deepened, and Sarah's hands began to wander. She ran them over Emily's body, feeling every curve and dip. Emily moaned, her fingers digging into Sarah's skin.

Sarah broke the kiss and trailed her lips down Emily's neck. Emily tilted her head back, giving Sarah better access. Sarah sucked and nibbled at Emily's neck, leaving a trail of kisses behind.

Emily's hands were now busy, unbuttoning Sarah's shirt. Sarah helped her, shrugging out of the shirt and tossing it aside. Emily's eyes widened as she took in Sarah's lacy bra.

Sarah reached behind her and unclasped her bra, letting it fall away. Emily's eyes were glued to Sarah's breasts, and Sarah could feel her nipples harden under Emily's gaze.

Emily leaned forward and took one of Sarah's nipples into her mouth. Sarah moaned, her head falling back. Emily sucked and licked at Sarah's nipple, her hands wandering down to Sarah's pants.

She undid Sarah's pants and slipped her hand inside. Sarah was already wet, and Emily groaned as she felt how slick Sarah was.

Sarah's hand was now in Emily's hair, pulling gently. Emily looked up at her, and Sarah could see the desire in her eyes.

"Fuck me," Sarah whispered.

Emily didn't need to be asked twice. She stood up, pulling Sarah with her. Sarah wrapped her legs around Emily's waist, and Emily carried her to the bedroom.

Emily laid Sarah down on the bed and pulled off her pants. Sarah was now completely naked, and Emily couldn't help but stare.

Emily quickly undressed and climbed onto the bed. She positioned herself between Sarah's legs and leaned down to kiss her.

As they kissed, Emily's fingers found Sarah's clit. Sarah moaned, her hips bucking up to meet Emily's fingers. Emily rubbed slow circles around Sarah's clit, building her pleasure.

Sarah's hands were now in Emily's hair, pulling and tugging. Emily loved it when Sarah got rough with her, and she could feel her own pleasure building.

Emily slipped a finger inside Sarah, and Sarah's moans grew louder. Emily added a second finger, and Sarah's hips began to move in time with Emily's fingers. Emily felt Sarah was more wet than usual and felt cum, but she ignored. Sarah understood that Emily felt cum and she also ignored.

Emily curled her fingers, hitting Sarah's G-spot. Sarah cried out, her orgasm crashing over her. Emily continued to rub Sarah's clit, drawing out her orgasm.

When Sarah's orgasm finally subsided, Emily pulled her fingers out and moved up to kiss Sarah. Sarah could taste herself on Emily's lips, and it only made her want more.

Emily reached into the bedside table and pulled out a wearable dildo. She wore it and positioned herself at Sarah's entrance and pushed inside. Sarah moaned, her hips meeting Emily's thrusts. This dick was bigger than Steves. Emily set a slow pace, building up their pleasure.

Sarah's legs were now wrapped around Emily's waist, and her hands were in Emily's hair. Emily leaned down to kiss Sarah, their tongues dancing together.

Emily's thrusts grew faster, and Sarah's moans grew louder. Emily could feel her own orgasm building, and she knew Sarah was close too.

Emily reached down between them and rubbed Sarah's clit. Sarah's orgasm hit her like a wave, and she cried out. Emily followed soon after, her orgasm ripping through her.

Emily collapsed on top of Sarah, both of them panting and sweating. Sarah ran her hands over Emily's back, feeling the muscles ripple under her fingers.

They lay like that for a few minutes, both of them lost in their own thoughts.

Finally, Sarah broke the silence. "That was amazing," she said.

Emily nodded. "Yeah, it was."

Sarah smiled. "I love you."

Emily smiled back. "I love you too."

Chapter 6: Brewing Tensions

As the days passed, Emily couldn't shake the growing sense of unease in her home. She watched as Sarah and James's interactions with Lisa seemed to become more frequent, and she couldn't help but feel increasingly sidelined. The tension in the house was palpable, a silent storm brewing beneath the surface.

One evening, Emily was in the kitchen, preparing dinner. The rhythmic chop of vegetables on the cutting board was the only sound, but her mind was a whirlwind of thoughts. Sarah walked in, her face glowing from another productive day spent working on her startup.

"Hey, Em. Need any help?" Sarah asked, her voice cheerful.

Emily glanced at her, forcing a smile. "No, I've got it. Thanks."

Sarah sensed the tension but chose to ignore it for now. She knew this conversation was inevitable, but she wasn't ready for it just yet. "Okay, I'll just set the table then."

A few minutes later, James walked in, his expression weary. "Hey, everyone. How was your day?"

"It was good," Sarah replied quickly, trying to keep the atmosphere light. "How about yours?"

"Busy, as usual," James said, giving Emily a quick kiss on the cheek before sitting down at the table. "Lisa called earlier. She needs some advice about her new job."

Emily's hand tightened around the knife she was holding. She took a deep breath before turning to face James. "She seems to need a lot of your advice lately."

James looked at her, confusion flickering in his eyes. "She's just going through a tough time. You know that."

"Does she really need to call you every day, though?" Emily asked, her voice edged with frustration.

Sarah intervened, trying to defuse the situation. "Em, Lisa's just trying to find her footing. She's not trying to cause any trouble."

Emily's gaze shifted to Sarah, her eyes narrowing slightly. "It's not just about Lisa, and you know it."

James looked between the two women, sensing the deeper undercurrent of tension. "What's really going on here?"

Emily set down the knife and leaned against the counter, her arms crossed. "I feel like I'm being sidelined. You and Sarah are so focused on your projects and Lisa, and I'm left here to handle everything else."

James's expression softened. "Emily, that's not true. We're just trying to support each other and Lisa."

Sarah stepped closer; her voice gentle but firm. "Emily, you're not being sidelined. We're all in this together. But if you're feeling overwhelmed, we need to talk about it."

Emily shook her head, her frustration boiling over. "Talking doesn't seem to change anything. Actions speak louder, and right now, the actions show that I'm not a priority."

The room fell silent, the weight of Emily's words hanging heavily in the air. James and Sarah exchanged a worried glance, realizing the depth of Emily's feelings.

"I'm sorry you feel that way, Em," James said quietly. "We'll do better. I promise."

Sarah nodded, her eyes filled with sincerity. "We'll figure this out, Emily. We don't want you to feel like this."

Emily looked at them both, her heart aching. She wanted to believe them, but the constant interactions with Lisa and the focus on their projects made it hard. She needed to see real change, not just hear promises.

That night, as they lay in bed, Emily turned to James. "Do you think we're making the right choices? With everything?"

James sighed, pulling her closer. "I don't know, Emily. But I do know that I love you, and I'm committed to making this work. For all of us."

Emily rested her head on his chest, feeling the steady beat of his heart. "I just want us to be happy. Together."

"We will be," James murmured, his voice filled with determination. "We'll find a way."

Meanwhile, Sarah lay awake in her own bed, her mind racing. She couldn't ignore the growing distance between her and Emily. She knew she had to step up and show Emily that she was still a priority. But she also couldn't deny the thrill of her startup and the support she was receiving from Steve.

The next day, Sarah made a conscious effort to spend more time with Emily. They went for a walk in the park, the crisp autumn air filled with the scent of fallen leaves. They talked about their plans, their dreams, and their fears, trying to reconnect.

"I'm sorry if I've been distant," Sarah said, her voice sincere. "I've been so caught up in everything, and I didn't realize how it was affecting you."

Emily looked at her, appreciating the effort. "I just need to feel like I'm part of this, Sarah. Not an outsider."

"You're not an outsider," Sarah replied, taking Emily's hand. "You're the heart of this family. And I'll do everything I can to make sure you feel that."

As the weeks passed by, the tension slowly began to ease. Emily saw the effort that James and Sarah were making, and she started to feel more included. But there was still an underlying current of unease, a sense that things weren't quite settled.

One evening, as they sat together, Sarah received a text from Steve. She glanced at it, her heart skipping a beat. Emily noticed, her eyes narrowing slightly.

"Who's that?" Emily asked, trying to keep her tone casual.

"Just Steve," Sarah replied, a bit too quickly. "He wanted to check on the progress of the startup."

Emily nodded, not entirely convinced. She knew there was more to the story, but she decided to let it go for now. She needed to trust that Sarah would come to her when she was ready.

As the weeks went by, the dynamics in their household continued to shift. James and Sarah's interactions with Lisa and Steve remained a point of tension, but they all worked to communicate better and support each other.

Despite the brewing tensions, there was a sense of determination. They were committed to making their unconventional family work, navigating the complexities of their relationships with honesty and love. And as they faced each new challenge, they knew that together, they could weather storm, hopefully.

Chapter 7: Confession

The atmosphere in the house had become increasingly tense, with Emily feeling more sidelined each day. She couldn't ignore the feeling that Sarah had ulterior motives, and it was time to confront her. The final straw came one evening when Emily noticed Sarah receiving another text from Steve, her face lighting up in a way that Emily hadn't seen in a long time.

Emily waited until James had gone out for a walk. She found Sarah in the living room, scrolling through her phone. Taking a deep breath, Emily sat down across from her, determination etched on her face.

"Sarah, we need to talk," Emily began, her voice steady but filled with resolve.

Sarah looked up, sensing the gravity of Emily's tone. She put her phone down, giving Emily her full attention. "What's going on, Em?"

Emily's eyes narrowed slightly. "I've been feeling like you've been distant, and I can't help but feel you're not being completely honest with me. What's really going on with you and Steve?"

Sarah's expression faltered for a moment before she straightened her shoulders. "Steve is just helping me with the startup. That's it."

"Is it really just that?" Emily pressed, her voice rising. "I see the way you light up when he texts you, and I can't ignore the fact that you're spending so much time away from home. It feels like you're trying to push me out."

Sarah's eyes flashed with frustration. "Emily, I'm not trying to push you out. I'm trying to build something for myself. Something I can be proud of."

Emily shook her head, tears welling up in her eyes. "It's more than that, Sarah. I can feel it. You're trying to take James away from me."

Sarah's face hardened, her voice cold. "Maybe because no one can love James better than me."

The words hung in the air, a heavy silence settling between them. Emily's heart pounded in her chest, a mix of anger and hurt coursing through her veins. "How can you say that? We're supposed to be a family. We're supposed to support each other."

"Supporting each other doesn't mean I have to sit back and watch you take everything I care about," Sarah shot back, her voice trembling with emotion. "James and I... we have a connection you can't understand."

Emily felt like the ground had shifted beneath her feet. "So, what? You're planning to take James away from me? Break up our family?"

Sarah's eyes softened for a moment, but her resolve remained. "I don't want to break up our family. But I can't deny my feelings for James. I love him, Emily. And I believe he loves me too."

Emily's voice cracked with pain. "And where does that leave me? Where does that leave us?"

Sarah looked away, unable to meet Emily's gaze. "I don't know. But I can't pretend anymore."

The room felt stifling, the weight of their argument pressing down on both of them. Emily stood up, her hands trembling. "This isn't fair, Sarah. We were supposed to be a team. How could you do this?"

Sarah's eyes filled with tears. "I didn't mean for it to happen, Emily. But I can't change how I feel."

Emily took a step back, her voice barely above a whisper. "I need some time to think."

She turned and walked out of the room, leaving Sarah sitting alone, tears streaming down her face. Emily's mind was a whirlwind of emotions as she made her way to their bedroom, the silence of the house amplifying her inner turmoil.

Hours later, James returned from his walk to find the house eerily quiet. He found Emily in their bedroom, sitting on the edge of the bed, her face streaked with tears. He immediately went to her, concern etched on his face.

"Emily, what's wrong?" James asked, his voice filled with worry.

Emily looked up at him, her heart aching. "We need to talk, James. About Sarah."

James sat down beside her, taking her hand in his. "What happened?"

Emily took a deep breath, trying to steady herself. "Sarah and I had a fight. She admitted she has feelings for you only. She said no one can love you better than her and her she was pretending feelings for me"

James's face paled, his eyes widening in shock. "What? That can't be true. Sarah and I... I truly love you Emily..."

"I believe you, James," Emily interrupted, her voice firm. "But this changes everything. We need to figure out what to do next."

James pulled her into his arms, holding her tightly. "We'll get through this, Emily. I promise. We'll find a way to make things right."

As they held each other, Emily felt a glimmer of hope. She knew the road ahead would be difficult, but she also knew that their love was strong enough to overcome any obstacle. Together, they would face the challenges that lay ahead, determined to rebuild their family and find a way forward.

Chapter 8: The Final Straw

The tension in the house had reached a breaking point. Emily's confrontation with Sarah had left a deep rift, and James found himself caught in the middle, torn between his love for both women. He couldn't deny the bond he shared with Sarah, but his heart belonged to Emily. He knew he had to make a difficult decision to restore peace in their home.

One evening, while Emily was out running errands, James decided to confront Sarah about her manipulative plans. He found her in the living room, scrolling through her phone with a distracted expression.

"Sarah, we need to talk," James said, his voice steady but firm.

Sarah looked up, sensing the seriousness in his tone. She put her phone down and nodded. "Alright, James. What's going on?"

James took a deep breath, his eyes locking onto hers. "I know about your plans to sideline Emily. I can't believe you would do something like that."

Sarah's eyes widened in surprise, but she quickly composed herself. "James, it's not what you think. I just... I wanted to find a way for us to be together."

"By hurting Emily?" James's voice was filled with frustration. "That's not the way to go about it, Sarah. I love Emily, and I can't let you come between us."

Sarah's expression hardened, her voice trembling with emotion. "You don't understand, James. No one can love you better than I do. I've been there for you through everything."

James shook his head, his heart aching. "I do understand, Sarah. But this isn't right. You're trying to manipulate the situation to your advantage, and it's tearing us apart."

Sarah's eyes filled with tears, but she quickly wiped them away. "So what are you saying, James? That you choose her over me?"

James looked at her, his expression resolute. "I choose peace, Sarah. I choose honesty. And right now, that means I have to step back from whatever this is between us."

Sarah's face fell, and for a moment, she looked vulnerable. "I never wanted it to come to this."

James sighed, his voice softening. "Neither did I. But we need to figure out a way to coexist without all this deception and manipulation."

Just then, the front door opened, and Emily walked in, carrying groceries. She sensed the tension in the room and paused, looking between James and Sarah.

"What's going on?" Emily asked, her voice cautious.

James turned to Emily, his eyes filled with determination. "Emily, there's something you need to know. Sarah has been trying to manipulate things to push you out."

Emily's eyes widened in shock, and she turned to Sarah. "Is that true?"

Sarah's face crumpled, and she nodded. "Yes, it's true. But I never wanted to hurt you, Emily."

Emily's heart ached, but she felt a sense of relief knowing the truth. "Why, Sarah? Why would you do this?"

Sarah's voice broke as she spoke. "Because I love James, and I thought I could make him happier than you could."

Emily shook her head, tears streaming down her face. "Love doesn't work like that, Sarah. You can't force it or manipulate it. It has to be genuine."

James stepped closer to Emily, taking her hand in his. "Emily, I promise you that my love for you is genuine. I'm so sorry for everything that's happened."

Emily looked at him, her heart filled with a mix of emotions. "I know, James. But this has to stop. We need to find a way to move forward without all this pain and deception."

Sarah stood there, feeling a mix of regret and sorrow. She knew she had crossed a line, and it was time to face the consequences.

As the days passed, Sarah began to distance herself, spending more time away from home. Emily couldn't shake the feeling that Sarah was hiding something. She decided to follow her one evening and discovered Sarah's secret Tinder life. The realization hit Emily hard, but it also gave her the clarity she needed.

One evening, Emily confronted Sarah once more. "Sarah, I know about your Tinder life. Why didn't you tell us?"

Sarah looked at Emily, her expression one of defeat. "I didn't think it mattered. I was just trying to find some happiness for myself."

Emily shook her head, her voice filled with sadness. "You can't keep living like this, Sarah. It's not fair to any of us."

Sarah sighed, her shoulders slumping. "I know. I just didn't know how to stop."

Emily reached out, taking Sarah's hand. "We can help you, but you have to be honest with us. No more secrets."

Sarah looked at Emily, tears filling her eyes. "Okay. No more secrets."

James joined them, his expression one of resolve. "We need to rebuild the trust between us. It's the only way we can move forward."

As they stood together, the weight of their decisions pressing down on them, they knew the road ahead would be difficult. But with honesty, love, and determination, they believed they could find a way to restore peace and happiness in their home.

The next morning, as the sun rose over their house, Emily, James, and Sarah sat down together, ready to face the challenges ahead. They knew it wouldn't be easy, but they were committed to making it work, one step at a time.

Chapter 9: Breaking Point

The air in the house was thick with tension. The recent revelations about Sarah had left James and Emily reeling, their trust shattered. James had just discovered that Sarah had been meeting with her past lover, Steve, multiple times. This, coupled with her secret Tinder dealings, was the final straw.

James was pacing the living room, his face a storm of emotions. Emily sat on the couch, her hands clasped tightly in her lap. She watched James, her heart breaking for him.

"James, we need to talk to Sarah," Emily said, her voice steady despite the turmoil inside her.

James stopped pacing and looked at her, his eyes filled with a mixture of anger and pain. "I can't believe she would do this. After everything we've been through."

Emily stood up, walking over to him. She placed a hand on his arm, offering comfort. "We'll get through this, James. Together."

Just then, Sarah walked into the room, sensing the tension immediately. "What's going on?" she asked, her voice wary.

James turned to face her, his expression hardening. "Sarah, we need to talk. Now."

Sarah's eyes widened, but she nodded, sitting down on the couch. "Okay. What is it?"

James took a deep breath, trying to control his anger. "I know about your meetings with Steve. And your Tinder life. How could you do this to us?"

Sarah's face paled, and she looked down, unable to meet his gaze. "James, I... I'm sorry. I never meant for things to get so out of hand."

Emily stepped forward, her voice firm. "We trusted you, Sarah. We believed in you. But you've been lying to us, manipulating us. This has to stop."

Sarah's eyes filled with tears, her voice trembling. "I know I've made mistakes. I was just trying to find some happiness for myself."

James shook his head, his voice cold. "At our expense? You've hurt us, Sarah. And you've hurt yourself."

Sarah's tears spilled over, and she looked up at them, her face filled with regret. "I didn't know what else to do. I felt so alone."

Emily's heart softened slightly, but she knew they had to be firm. "We want to help you, Sarah. But you need to be honest with us. No more secrets. No more lies."

Sarah nodded, wiping away her tears. "I promise. No more secrets."

James took a deep breath, his voice steady. "We need to take action, Sarah. You need to end things with Steve and delete your Tinder account. You need to focus on rebuilding trust with us."

Sarah looked at him, her eyes filled with determination. "I will. I'll do whatever it takes."

Emily stepped forward, placing a hand on Sarah's shoulder. "We're here for you, Sarah. But this is your last chance. You need to prove to us that you're willing to change."

Sarah nodded; her voice filled with emotion. "I will. I promise."

As the days passed, Sarah made a concerted effort to rebuild their trust. She ended things with Steve, deleted her Tinder account, and focused on repairing her relationship with James and Emily. It wasn't easy, and there were moments of tension and doubt, but they were committed to working through it together. Sarah internally knew that the Tinder account she deleted in front of them was a secondary one. She just wanted to get over this situation.

One evening, as they sat together in the living room, James turned to Sarah. "I'm proud of you, Sarah. You've taken the first steps toward making things right."

Sarah looked at him, her eyes filled with gratitude. "Thank you, James. I know I have a long way to go, but I'm determined to make things right."

Emily nodded, her voice gentle. "We believe in you, Sarah. We're here to support you."

As they sat together, the weight of the past few weeks began to lift. They knew they still had a long way to go, but they were committed to facing the challenges ahead with honesty and love. Together, they would rebuild their family, stronger and more united than ever before.

Chapter 10: Goodbye, Sarah

The air was crisp as Emily walked out of the Target parking lot, her arms filled with shopping bags. She noticed a familiar figure entering a nearby hotel, and her heart skipped a beat. It was Sarah. Emily's instincts kicked in, and she decided to follow her, curiosity and suspicion gnawing at her.

Emily slipped into the hotel lobby, keeping a safe distance. She watched as Sarah met Steve, her old lover, who was in town for a business trip. They exchanged a brief conversation before heading towards the elevator. Emily's heart pounded as she trailed them, staying out of sight.

Sarah and Steve entered a grand suite on the fifth floor, and Emily's worst fears were confirmed. She felt a mix of anger and betrayal boiling inside her. She quickly pulled out her phone and texted James, her fingers trembling.

"James, come to the hotel near Target. I need you here. Now."

Steve and Sarah were nestled in a plush hotel suite on the fifth floor with no idea what was in store for Sarah, the scent sof fresh paper and ink still lingering in the air. After weeks of negotiations, they had finally signed the contract that would fund Sarah's groundbreaking startup. As they shared a toast to their new beginning, Steve couldn't help but admire Sarah's determination and intelligence.

Sarah, in turn, found herself increasingly drawn to Steve's charm and wit now that she got the funding. She realized that their connection went beyond business; they shared a spark that couldn't be ignored. After couple of drinks, the conversation became flirtatious, and they found themselves lingering on each other's words, their eyes locked in a magnetic dance.

"I've been thinking about you all day, Steve," Sarah admitted, her voice barely above a whisper.

"Have you now?" Steve replied, a smile playing at the corners of his lips. "I can't deny that you've been on my mind, too."

The tension between them was palpable as Sarah moved closer, her hand resting softly on Steve's chest. He gently stroked her cheek, his thumb tracing her lower lip as he leaned in for a kiss. Their lips met in a passionate exchange, their tongues dancing together in a rhythm as old as time.

As they broke apart, Steve whispered, "Let's take this to the bedroom."

Sarah nodded, her eyes glistening with desire. Once in the bedroom, they slowly undressed each other, their hands exploring every inch of skin they exposed. Sarah marveled at Steve's toned physique, while he admired the curves of her body.

Foreplay began with soft kisses on the lips, gradually moving to the neck and earlobes. Steve's fingers traced the outline of Sarah's lace bra, teasing her nipples to hard peaks. Sarah responded by unbuttoning Steve's shirt, her fingers running over his muscular chest and abs.

Their hands wandered lower, caressing each other's inner thighs and teasing the edges of their underwear. Sarah, unable to resist any longer, slipped her hand into Steve's boxers, wrapping her fingers around his firm cock. Steve let out a low moan as Sarah began to stroke him, her thumb gliding over the tip of his shaft.

Steve, in turn, slid his hand into Sarah's panties, finding her wet and ready for him. He gently circled her clit with his fingers, causing Sarah to gasp and writhe in pleasure.

"Fuck, Steve, I need you inside me," Sarah begged, her voice husky with desire.

Steve didn't hesitate, removing his boxers and positioning himself at Sarah's entrance. He teased her, rubbing the head of his cock against her clit before slowly pushing inside her. Sarah's back arched as she took him in, her breath hitching with each inch he claimed.

Once Steve was fully seated, they began to move together, their bodies finding a natural rhythm. Sarah's moans filled the room, mingling with Steve's grunts as they chased their release.

"Harder, Steve, harder," Sarah demanded, her nails digging into Steve's back.

Steve obliged, driving into her with renewed intensity. Sarah wrapped her legs around his waist, meeting his thrusts with equal fervor. As they approached their climax, Steve reached down to rub Sarah's clit, sending her over the edge.

"Oh, fuck, Steve! Yes, yes, yes!" Sarah cried out, her pussy clenching around Steve's cock as she came.

Steve wasn't far behind, his own orgasm crashing through him as he emptied himself inside Sarah. They collapsed onto the bed, their bodies slick with sweat and utterly spent.

As they caught their breath, Steve whispered in Sarah's ear, "I think we've earned another toast."

Sarah smiled, her arms encircling Steve's waist. "I'll drink to that." The room doorbell rang thinking must be room service. Sarah got up from the bed and wrapped a white towel covering her breasts and body. Steve looked at her and admired her body.

James arrived within 30 minutes; his face etched with concern. Emily met him in the lobby, her eyes filled with unshed tears. "She's here, with Steve. They went into a room together."

James's jaw tightened, and he took a deep breath. "Let's go confront her."

They took the elevator to the fifth floor, and Emily led James to the room she had seen Sarah enter. With a firm knock, they waited.

Moments later, Sarah opened the door, her face paling when she saw them, wearing only a towel.

"Emily, James, what are you doing here?" Sarah stammered, trying to block the doorway.

Emily's voice was steady, but her eyes were blazing with hurt. "We need to talk, Sarah. Now."

Sarah stepped aside, letting them in. Steve was sitting on the edge of the bed with just boxers, looking uncomfortable. Emily and James stood in the center of the room, facing Sarah.

"Sarah, we trusted you," James began, his voice filled with a mixture of anger and disappointment. "You promised no more secrets, no more lies. But here you are, meeting Steve behind our backs."

Sarah's eyes welled up with tears, and she looked away, unable to meet their gaze. "I... I'm sorry. I didn't know how to stop. I needed the funding for my startup, and I... I fell back into old habits."

Emily shook her head, her voice breaking. "This isn't just about the funding, Sarah. It's about trust, and you've shattered it. How could you do this to us? To our family?"

Sarah's shoulders slumped, and she wiped her tears. "I never meant to hurt you. I just felt so lost and alone."

James's voice was firm, but there was a hint of sadness. "We can't keep doing this, Sarah. We can't keep living with this betrayal. You need to leave today from our house."

Sarah looked up, her eyes wide with shock and despair. "James, please. I can change. I can make things right."

Emily's voice softened, but there was a finality to her words. "We've given you chances, Sarah. But you keep breaking our trust. You need to go."

Steve stood up wearing his robe, sensing the gravity of the situation. "I'll leave you to talk," he said quietly, heading for the door.

After Steve left, the room was filled with a heavy silence. Sarah looked at Emily and James, her heart breaking. "I'm so sorry. I never wanted it to come to this."

James nodded, his eyes filled with a mixture of pain and resolve. "It's time for us to move on, Sarah. You need to find your own path, and we need to heal."

Emily stepped forward; her eyes filled with unshed tears. "I wish you all the best, Sarah. I hope you find the happiness you're looking for."

Sarah nodded, her voice barely a whisper.

Sarah came in the evening and packed her things and left their home, the weight of her departure settled on Emily and James. They knew it would take time to heal, but they were committed to rebuilding their trust and love.

That evening, as they sat together on the couch, Emily leaned her head on James's shoulder. "Do you think we'll be okay?"

James wrapped his arm around her, his voice filled with determination. "I know we will, Emily. We'll get through this, together."

Emily nodded, feeling a sense of peace despite the pain. "Together."

As they watched the sunset from their living room, they knew that the road ahead would be challenging. But with honesty, love, and unwavering support, they believed they could overcome any obstacle and find their way back to each other.

Chapter 11: Picking Up the Pieces

The departure of Sarah had left a void in the house, but it also marked a new beginning for Emily and James. Determined to rebuild their relationship, they decided to take a much-needed vacation to an adults-only resort in Mexico, hoping to find a new sense of normalcy and reconnect on a deeper level. Emily's mother gladly agreed to take care of Max, giving Emily and James the space they needed.

As they arrived at the resort, the warm sun and gentle ocean breeze welcomed them. The resort was a paradise, with lush gardens, serene pools, and a private beach that stretched as far as the eye could see. Emily and James checked into their luxurious suite, which overlooked the ocean, and felt a wave of relief and excitement wash over them.

"This place is beautiful," Emily said, her eyes wide with wonder as she took in the view from their balcony.

"It really is," James agreed, wrapping his arms around her from behind. "I think this is exactly what we needed."

They spent their first few days lounging by the pool, exploring the resort, and indulging in the exquisite cuisine. The stress and tension that had plagued them began to melt away, replaced by a sense of peace and renewal. One afternoon, they decided to try a couples' meditation class that the resort offered.

In a tranquil, open-air pavilion surrounded by tropical plants, they sat on comfortable mats, guided by a soft-spoken instructor. The meditation session helped them to quiet their minds and focus on their connection with each other. As they breathed in unison, they felt a deep sense of calm and unity.

After the session, James turned to Emily, his eyes filled with love and gratitude. "This is amazing. I feel like we're finally starting to find ourselves again."

Emily smiled, squeezing his hand. "I feel it too. I'm so glad we came here."

The next day, they decided to try a Tantra massage workshop. The experience was both intimate and enlightening, teaching them how to connect on a deeper, more spiritual level. They learned techniques to enhance their intimacy and communication, and the workshop brought them even closer together.

James and Emily returned from Tantra massage workshop at the resort to the room to take shower. The sensual touches, deep breathing exercises, and mindful connection had left them both feeling incredibly aroused. As they entered their room, their eyes locked, and they knew that they were in for a day of passion and pleasure.

"Mmm, Emily, you look absolutely stunning," James said, his voice low and husky.

"And you're not so bad yourself," Emily replied, her eyes sparkling with desire.

James stepped closer to Emily, his arms encircling her waist. He leaned in, his lips meeting hers in a slow, sensual kiss. Their tongues danced together as they explored each other's mouths, their hands roaming over each other's bodies.

"I want you, Emily," James whispered in her ear. "I want to make love to you all day long."

Emily shivered with anticipation. "Take me to the shower," she said, her voice trembling with desire.

James led Emily to the bathroom, turning on the water and adjusting the temperature. They stepped under the warm spray, their bodies slick with soap and water. James's hands roamed over Emily's curves, his fingers teasing her nipples and tracing the lines of her body.

"You're so beautiful," he murmured, his lips finding hers once again.

Emily moaned with pleasure as James's hands explored her body. She could feel his erection pressing against her hip, and she reached down to stroke him.

"Oh, James," she whispered, her fingers encircling his hard length. "I want you inside me."

James growled with desire, lifting Emily up and pressing her against the shower wall. She wrapped her legs around his waist, her arms around his neck as he entered her.

"Fuck, Emily, you feel amazing," he groaned, his hips thrusting against hers.

Emily moaned with pleasure, her nails digging into James's shoulders as he filled her. She rocked her hips against his, their bodies moving in perfect harmony.

"Yes, James, just like that," she gasped, her orgasm building inside her.

James could feel Emily's muscles tightening around him, and he knew she was close. He thrust harder and faster, his own orgasm building inside him.

"Come for me, Emily," he growled, his lips finding hers once again.

Emily moaned as she came, her orgasm rippling through her body. James followed her over the edge, his own release exploding from him.

They stayed there, locked together, as the water rained down on them. Finally, they pulled apart, their bodies slick with sweat and cum.

"That was incredible," Emily murmured, her eyes shining with happiness.

"It certainly was," James agreed, smiling down at her. "But I'm not done with you yet."

Emily's eyes sparkled with desire. "Oh, really?" she said, her voice low and husky.

James nodded, lifting Emily up and carrying her to the bed. He laid her down on the soft sheets, his body covering hers.

"I want to explore every inch of you," he murmured, his lips finding hers once again.

Emily moaned with pleasure as James's lips trailed down her body. He licked and nibbled at her neck, his fingers teasing her nipples. She could feel his erection pressing against her hip, and she reached down to stroke him.

"Oh, James, you feel so good," she moaned, her hips rocking against his.

James growled with desire, his lips finding her nipples. He sucked and teased them, his fingers tracing the lines of her body. Emily moaned with pleasure, her hips rocking against his.

James could feel Emily's arousal building once again, and he knew he had to taste her. He moved down her body, his lips finding her wet folds. He licked and sucked at her clit, his fingers teasing her entrance.

"Oh, yes, James, just like that," Emily moaned, her hips thrusting against his face.

James could feel Emily's orgasm building once again, and he knew he had to be inside her. He reached for the condom on the nightstand, rolling it onto his hard length. He positioned himself at her entrance, his eyes meeting hers.

"I'm going to make you scream with pleasure, Emily," he growled, his hips thrusting forward.

Emily moaned with pleasure as James filled her once again. He thrust hard and fast, his hips slapping against hers. She could feel another orgasm building inside her, and she reached down to stroke her clit.

"Yes, James, harder," she gasped, her hips thrusting against his.

James growled with desire, his hips thrusting harder and faster. He could feel his own orgasm building inside him, and he knew he couldn't hold back much longer.

"Come for me, Emily," he groaned, his fingers teasing her clit.

Emily moaned as she came, her orgasm rippling through her body. James followed her over the edge, his own release exploding from him.

They lay there, spent and satisfied, as their breathing slowed.

"That was amazing," Emily murmured, her eyes shining with happiness.

"It certainly was," James agreed, smiling down at her. "But I'm still not done with you yet."

Emily's eyes sparkled with desire. "Oh, really?" she said, her voice low and husky.

James nodded, his lips finding hers once again.

"Let's explore every position in the book," he murmured, his hips thrusting against hers.

That evening, as they sat on the beach, watching the sunset, Emily rested her head on James's shoulder. "I feel like we're healing, James. This place, this time together, it's helping us."

James nodded, his voice soft and filled with emotion. "We needed this, Em. We needed to remember why we fell in love in the first place."

They sat in comfortable silence for a while, the sound of the waves creating a soothing backdrop. Then James spoke, his voice thoughtful. "What do you think about our future? How do we move forward from here?"

Emily took a deep breath, considering his question. "I think we need to keep being honest with each other. No more secrets, no more letting things fester. We need to communicate and support each other, no matter what."

James nodded, his hand gently stroking her hair. "I agree. We've been through so much, but I believe we can come out stronger on the other side. I want us to build a life together that's filled with love and trust."

Emily looked up at him, her eyes shining with determination. "I want that too. I want us to create a home that's full of happiness and understanding. We deserve that."

James leaned down, pressing a tender kiss to her forehead. "We do. And we'll make it happen, together."

Their days at the resort were filled with relaxation, adventure, and deep conversations. They went snorkeling, explored local markets, and danced under the stars. Each experience brought them closer, helping them to rebuild their bond and create new memories.

On their last night at the resort, they had a romantic dinner on the beach, the table set with candles and surrounded by soft lanterns. As they enjoyed their meal, they talked about their hopes and dreams for the future.

"I feel so grateful to have you in my life," James said, his voice filled with sincerity. "You're my rock, Emily."

Emily smiled, reaching across the table to take his hand. "And you're mine, James. I love you more than words can say."

As the moon rose over the ocean, casting a silvery glow on the water, they knew they were ready to face whatever challenges lay ahead. They had found a new sense of normalcy, a renewed commitment to each other, and a deeper understanding of their love.

When they returned home, they felt rejuvenated and ready to continue their journey together. Max greeted them with open arms, and Emily's mother was happy to see the newfound light in their eyes.

Emily and James knew that their path wouldn't always be easy, but they were determined to face it together, with honesty, love, and unwavering support. They had picked up the pieces of their relationship and were ready to build something even stronger, one day at a time.

Chapter 12: Lingering Doubts

Back home, the tranquility of their vacation in Mexico had faded into the background. Weeks passed, and despite their efforts to rebuild trust, Emily couldn't shake her doubts about James's loyalty. Her mind kept returning to his interactions with Lisa, and a gnawing suspicion took root in her heart.

One evening, as James prepared for another business trip to Seattle, Emily felt her resolve harden. She needed answers. "James, can we talk?" she asked, her voice steady but her heart racing.

James turned to her, sensing the seriousness in her tone. "Of course, Emily. What's on your mind?"

Emily took a deep breath, trying to keep her emotions in check. "I've been trying to trust you, but I can't help feeling uneasy about your trips to Seattle and Vegas. Especially when it comes to Lisa. I need to know the truth, James."

James's face softened, but there was a flicker of defensiveness in his eyes. "Emily, I've told you, those trips are for work. And Lisa... she's been going through a tough time. I'm just trying to help her."

Emily shook her head, her frustration bubbling to the surface. "It's more than that, James. I've seen the way she looks at you, and I know you've been secretive. I need to know what's really going on."

James sighed, running a hand through his hair. "Emily, I promise you, there's nothing more to it. You have to trust me."

But trust was a fragile thing, and Emily's doubts wouldn't be so easily assuaged. The next morning, after James left for his trip, Emily made a decision. She booked a flight to Vegas in secrecy, determined to uncover the truth.

When she arrived in Vegas, she checked into a hotel near the one James had mentioned in passing. Her heart pounded as she navigated the bustling city, her mind racing with possibilities. That evening, she made her way to the hotel lobby, her eyes scanning the crowd.

And then she saw them. James and Lisa, sitting together at a corner table in the hotel bar. They were laughing, their heads close together, an intimacy between them that made Emily's heart ache. She felt a surge of anger and betrayal, but she forced herself to stay calm. She needed to confront them both.

She approached their table, her voice steady despite the storm raging inside her. "James. Lisa. We need to talk."

James looked up, his face paling as he saw Emily. "Emily, what are you doing here?"

Lisa's eyes widened in shock, but she quickly composed herself. "Emily, this isn't what it looks like."

Emily shook her head, her voice trembling with emotion. "Save it, Lisa. I've seen enough. James, how could you do this to me? To us?"

James stood up, reaching out to her. "Emily, please, let me explain."

Emily took a step back, her eyes filled with tears. "Explain what, James? That you've been lying to me? That you've been seeing Lisa behind my back?"

James's shoulders slumped, and he looked down, unable to meet her gaze. "Emily, I'm so sorry. It started as just helping her, but things got out of hand. I didn't mean for it to happen."

Emily's heart broke at his words, but she forced herself to stay strong. "And you, Lisa? I thought you were my friend."

Lisa's face was filled with regret. "I'm sorry, Emily. I never wanted to hurt you. I just... I don't know. I got caught up in everything."

Emily took a deep breath, her voice filled with a mixture of pain and determination. "I deserve better than this. We all do. James, if you have any respect for me, you'll come home with me now and end this."

James looked at Lisa, then back at Emily, his eyes filled with sorrow. "Emily, I'm so sorry. I'll come home with you. I want to make things right."

As they left the hotel, the weight of betrayal hung heavy between them. The flight home was filled with a tense silence, both of them lost in their thoughts. When they finally arrived back at their house, Emily turned to James, her eyes filled with tears.

"James, I need you to be honest with me from now on. No more lies, no more secrets. If we're going to rebuild this, I need to trust you."

James nodded, his voice filled with sincerity. "I promise, Emily. I'll do whatever it takes to earn your trust back."

They stood together in the dimly lit living room, the echoes of their past mistakes lingering in the air. But there was also a glimmer of hope, a sense that maybe, just maybe, they could find a way to heal and move forward.

Emily took James's hand, her voice soft but firm. "We'll get through this, James. One step at a time."

James squeezed her hand, his eyes filled with determination. "Together, Emily. We'll do it together."

As they faced the uncertain future, they knew the road ahead would be difficult. But with honesty, love, and a renewed commitment to each other, they believed they could overcome the challenges and rebuild their relationship, one step at a time.

Chapter 13: The Path to Healing

The air in the house was heavy with unspoken words and unresolved emotions. Emily and James had reached a point where they knew they had to face their issues head-on if they wanted to rebuild their relationship. The wounds were deep, but they were determined to heal together.

One evening, after dinner, Emily sat down with James in the living room. The soft glow of the lamp cast a warm light, creating a cozy yet serious atmosphere.

"James, we need to talk," Emily began, her voice steady but filled with emotion.

James looked at her, sensing the gravity of the moment. "I know, Emily. There's a lot we need to discuss."

Emily took a deep breath, gathering her thoughts. "I've been holding something back. I need to be honest with you. After everything that happened with Sarah and Lisa, I felt hurt and betrayed. And in a moment of weakness, I saw Mark a few times."

James's eyes widened in surprise, a mixture of shock and pain crossing his face. "Mark? Emily, why?"

Emily's eyes filled with tears. "It wasn't about love, James. It was about revenge. I wanted to hurt you the way I felt hurt. But it was wrong, and I regret it deeply."

James sighed, running a hand through his hair. "Emily, I've made so many mistakes. I've been dishonest, and I've let you down. We've both hurt each other, and it's tearing us apart."

Emily reached out, taking his hand. "I think we need help. We can't do this alone. I want us to seek counseling, to really work through our issues and make a renewed commitment to each other."

James nodded, his eyes filled with determination. "I agree, Emily. We need to rebuild our trust and our love. Let's do it."

The next week, they found themselves in the comforting office of Dr. Anderson, their new counselor. The room was filled with soft, calming colors and the scent of lavender, creating an atmosphere of safety and openness.

"Thank you both for coming," Dr. Anderson began, her voice warm and inviting. "The fact that you're here shows your commitment to each other and to healing."

James spoke first, his voice filled with sincerity. "I've been dishonest with Emily. I've hurt her deeply, and I'm truly sorry. I want to make things right."

Emily squeezed his hand, her voice steady. "And I've made mistakes too. I've let my hurt guide my actions, and I saw someone else to get back at James. I regret it, and I want to move forward together."

Dr. Anderson nodded, her eyes understanding. "Many marriages face challenges, but the key to overcoming them is communication, trust, and a willingness to forgive. It's important to understand why these actions hurt and to find ways to rebuild your connection."

They spent the session discussing their feelings, guided by Dr. Anderson's thoughtful questions and advice. She helped them identify the underlying issues and gave them tools to improve their communication and rebuild their trust.

"Marriage requires continuous effort and understanding," Dr. Anderson explained. "You need to be honest with each other, even when it's difficult. Trust is rebuilt through consistent, positive actions over time."

James nodded, his voice filled with determination. "I understand that now. I promise to be honest and open."

Emily looked at him, her eyes softening. "And I promise to listen and to work on understanding your perspective."

Dr. Anderson encouraged them to practice these new skills at home and to continue attending sessions regularly. As they left her office, they felt a renewed sense of hope and determination.

That evening, they decided to try a Tantra meditation class, hoping to deepen their connection. The studio was serene, filled with the soft glow of candles and the soothing scent of incense. Rosy, the instructor, welcomed them warmly.

"Welcome, Emily and James," Rosy greeted them with a gentle smile. "Tantra meditation is about connecting with each other on a deeper level, finding balance and harmony."

They sat on cushions, facing each other, as Rosy guided them through the meditation. Her voice was calming, encouraging them to focus on their breath and the energy between them. They held hands, their eyes locked, feeling a sense of peace and unity.

"Feel the connection between you," Rosy instructed. "Breathe together, move together, and let your hearts align."

As they followed her guidance, Emily and James felt a renewed sense of closeness. The meditation helped them to quiet their minds and focus on the love they shared. They felt a deep sense of calm and connection, a reminder of why they had fallen in love in the first place.

After the class, Rosy spoke to them privately. "Remember, this journey is about being present with each other, finding joy in the small moments, and building a foundation of trust and love."

James nodded, his voice filled with gratitude. "Thank you, Rosy. This has been incredible."

Emily smiled, feeling a sense of peace. "We'll keep practicing and working on our connection."

As they left the studio, hand in hand, they felt a renewed sense of hope and determination. They knew the road ahead would be challenging, but they were committed to healing and rebuilding their relationship.

In the weeks that followed, they continued their counseling sessions and Tantra meditation classes. They practiced the tools and techniques they had learned, finding new ways to connect and communicate. Their home began to feel like a sanctuary once more, filled with love and understanding.

One evening, as they sat together on their porch, watching the sunset, Emily looked at James, her eyes filled with warmth. "I feel like we're finally finding our way back to each other."

James smiled, his heart swelling with love. "I feel it too, Emily. I love you more than ever."

Emily leaned in, pressing a tender kiss to his lips. "I love you too, James. We'll get through this, together."

As they held each other, they knew that the journey of healing and rebuilding trust would take time, but they were ready to face it, one step at a time, with love and unwavering commitment.

Chapter 14: Embracing the Future

JAMES AND EMILY HAD been exploring their spirituality together for the past year. They had attended numerous workshops and retreats, deepened their connection and learning new practices to enhance their relationship. One workshop they had recently attended focused on meditation, tantra, and the art of sacred sexuality. Eager to apply what they had learned, they decided to start their day with a morning meditation and tantric sex session.

As the sun began to rise, James and Emily sat cross-legged on their yoga mats, facing each other. They closed their eyes and began to focus on their breath, syncing their inhales and exhales as they connected with their partner on a deeper level. Emily opened her eyes and looked into James's, seeing the love and adoration reflected back at her. She felt a surge of desire and leaned in to kiss him gently, their lips meeting in a soft, sensual dance.

The kiss deepened as their hands began to explore each other's bodies. James traced his fingers along Emily's neck, feeling her heart race beneath his touch. She moaned softly, her breath hitching as he cupped her breast, his thumb flicking over her nipple. Emily arched into him, her own hands wandering down to James's cock, feeling it harden beneath her touch.

"Mmm, someone's ready for me," Emily purred, her voice low and sultry.

James grinned, his eyes darkening with desire. "Always, for you, my love."

Emily stood up, pulling James with her. She led him to their bed, their lips never breaking apart as they stumbled towards it. James pushed her down onto the mattress, his body covering hers as he continued to kiss her deeply. His hands roamed over her body, his touch setting her skin on fire.

"Fuck, James, I need you inside me," Emily gasped, her hips grinding up against him.

James didn't need any more encouragement. He reached down between their bodies, his fingers finding Emily's wet and ready for him. He teased her clit, feeling her shiver beneath him as he slid a finger inside her.

"Yes, oh god, yes," Emily moaned, her back arching off the bed.

James added a second finger, stretching her as he prepared her for his cock. He could feel her muscles clenching around him, ready for more. He pulled his fingers out, replacing them with his cock. He slid in slowly, savoring the feeling of her tight pussy swallowing him whole.

Once he was fully seated inside her, James paused, looking into Emily's eyes. "I love you," he whispered.

Emily smiled, her eyes shining with emotion. "I love you too, James."

With that, James began to move, his hips thrusting in a slow, steady rhythm. Emily matched him, meeting each thrust with one of her own.

Their breaths came in ragged gasps as they chased their pleasure, their bodies moving together in perfect harmony.

James reached down, his fingers finding Emily's clit once again. He rubbed slow circles around it, feeling her muscles clench around him as she got closer to her release.

"Oh god, James, I'm so close," Emily moaned, her hips bucking wildly.

James increased his pace, his fingers working her clit faster as he felt his own orgasm building. With one final thrust, he came hard, his cock pulsing inside Emily as she cried out her own release.

They lay there, panting and spent, their bodies slick with sweat. James pulled out, collapsing beside Emily on the bed.

"Wow," Emily breathed, her eyes wide with wonder. "That was...incredible."

James grinned, his arm snaking around her waist to pull her closer. "I told you tantric sex was mind-blowing."

Emily laughed, her head resting on his chest as they basked in the afterglow of their lovemaking.

As they lay there, their breaths slowly returning to normal, Emily looked up at James, her eyes sparkling with mischief.

"So, you think you can handle another round?" she asked, her hand already wandering down to James's cock.

James groaned, his hips thrusting up into her hand as he felt himself getting hard again.

"Challenge accepted," he replied, his lips meeting Emily's in another deep, passionate kiss.

Emily and James had decided to rebuild their relationship honestly, and the transformation was remarkable. Their bond had grown stronger, their trust had been restored, and they had found a deeper connection through their Tantra practices. The peace and stability they had worked so hard to achieve filled their home, creating an atmosphere of love and understanding.

One evening, as they sat together on the porch, watching the sunset, Emily leaned her head on James's shoulder. The warm glow of the setting sun bathed them in a golden light, and a gentle breeze rustled the leaves of the trees around them.

"It's amazing how far we've come," Emily said softly, her voice filled with gratitude. "I feel like we're closer than ever."

James smiled, wrapping his arm around her. "I feel the same way, Emily. Our journey hasn't been easy, but it's been worth it."

They sat in comfortable silence for a few moments, the sounds of the evening filling the air. Then James spoke, his tone thoughtful. "You know, I've been thinking about something. Our relationship has been incredibly spiritual and fulfilling, but sometimes I wonder if we should explore new experiences to keep things exciting."

Emily looked up at him, curiosity in her eyes. "What do you mean?"

James hesitated, then continued. "Well, I was thinking that maybe on our next vacation, we could try something different. Like hiring someone to spice things up a bit."

Emily raised an eyebrow, a playful smile tugging at her lips. "Are you suggesting we bring someone else into our relationship for a bit of fun?"

James chuckled, a little relieved that she wasn't completely dismissing the idea. "Yes, exactly. Just to try something new and exciting. But only if you're comfortable with it."

Emily thought for a moment, then nodded slowly. "I'm not averse to the idea. We've come a long way, and I trust you completely. It could be an interesting experience, as long as we're both on the same page and it doesn't affect our bond."

James kissed her forehead, his heart swelling with love for her. "I'm so grateful to have you in my life, Emily. We'll plan it carefully and make sure it's something we both enjoy."

They sat together, discussing the possibilities and making plans for their next vacation. They talked about the boundaries and rules they would set to ensure their relationship remained strong and their trust intact.

As the weeks went by, they continued their Tantra practices at home, finding new depths in their connection and intimacy. The spiritual aspect of their relationship had become a cornerstone, bringing them closer and allowing them to experience a profound sense of unity.

One Saturday afternoon, they decided to spend the day with Max, enjoying the simple pleasures of family life. They went to the park, played games, and had a picnic under the shade of a large oak tree. Max's laughter filled the air, and Emily and James felt a deep sense of contentment.

"Mom, Dad, this is the best day ever!" Max exclaimed, his eyes shining with joy.

Emily smiled, ruffling Max's hair. "We're glad you're having fun, sweetie. We love spending time with you."

James nodded; his heart full. "Family time is the best time."

As they watched Max chase after a butterfly, Emily turned to James, her eyes filled with love. "I'm so grateful for our family. We've been through so much, but it's made us stronger."

James squeezed her hand, his voice filled with emotion. "I couldn't agree more. We're in this together, now and always."

Their conversations about the future continued, and they made plans for their upcoming vacation. They talked openly about their desires and boundaries, ensuring that their relationship remained the priority.

When the time for their vacation finally arrived, they felt a mixture of excitement and anticipation. They had chosen a beautiful, secluded resort where they could relax and explore new experiences together.

As they stood on the balcony of their suite, overlooking the ocean, Emily leaned into James, her heart filled with hope and love. "Here's to new adventures and a future filled with love and trust."

James kissed her softly, his eyes shining with happiness. "Here's to us, Emily. We've come so far, and I know the best is yet to come."

As they embarked on their new adventure, they carried with them the lessons they had learned, the love they had nurtured, and the commitment they had made to each other. Their journey of healing had brought them closer than ever, and they were ready to embrace the future, hand in hand, with hearts open and spirits high.

About the Author

Candy Christie is an emerging author making her mark in the world of romance novels. With a few heartfelt books to her name, she has quickly captured the attention of readers who appreciate stories filled with emotional depth, vivid characters, and the timeless theme of love conquering all.

Growing up in a picturesque coastal town, Candy was inspired by the beauty around her and the rich tapestry of human experiences. This inspiration is evident in her writing, where she skillfully brings to life the settings and characters that resonate with authenticity and warmth. Her love for classic literature and a lifelong passion for storytelling led her to pursue a career in writing, where she finds joy in creating compelling narratives that touch the hearts of her readers.

Before embarking on her journey as a novelist, Candy worked in journalism, where she honed her skills in storytelling and character development. This background provided her with a strong foundation for her transition to writing fiction, allowing her to craft intricate plots and deeply relatable characters.

Candy's debut novel was met with enthusiasm from readers and critics alike, establishing her as a promising new voice in the romance genre. Her subsequent books have continued to build her reputation, each one showcasing her ability to weave together romance, suspense, and richly developed characters.

When she's not writing, Candy enjoys exploring the natural beauty of her hometown, painting, and spending time with her family and friends. She is also passionate about supporting literacy programs and inspiring a love of reading and writing in others.

Candy Christie's novels are a testament to the power of love, healing, and new beginnings. With each book, she invites readers to join her on a journey of passion and discovery, leaving them eagerly anticipating her next enchanting story.

About the Publisher